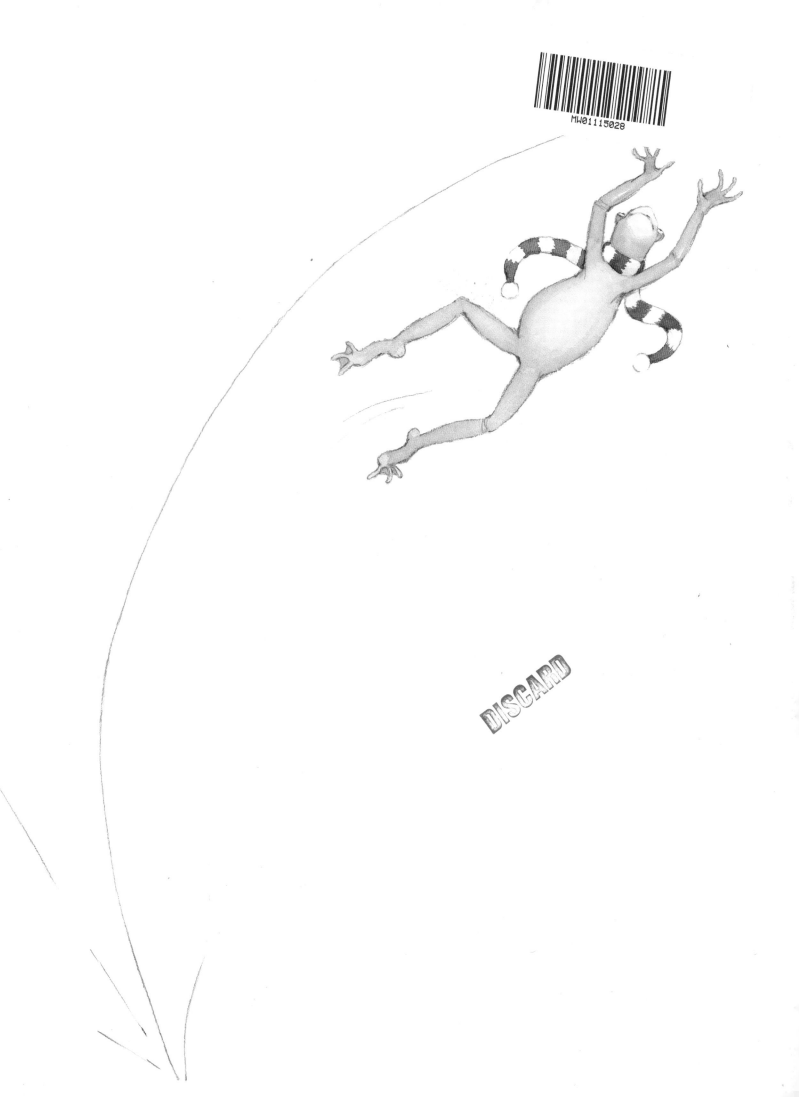

For Dri. I love you more than yesterday
and less than tomorrow
—S.T.

For D.P.D., my wonderful sister
—J.B.

DIAL BOOKS FOR YOUNG READERS
A division of Penguin Young Readers Group
Published by The Penguin Group
Penguin Group (USA) Inc., 375 Hudson Street, New York, NY 10014, U.S.A. • Penguin Group (Canada), 90 Eglinton Avenue East, Suite 700,
Toronto, Ontario, Canada M4P 2Y3 (a division of Pearson Penguin Canada Inc.) • Penguin Books Ltd, 80 Strand, London WC2R ORL, England
Penguin Ireland, 25 St. Stephen's Green, Dublin 2, Ireland (a division of Penguin Books Ltd) • Penguin Group (Australia), 250 Camberwell
Road, Camberwell, Victoria 3124, Australia • (a division of Pearson Australia Group Pty Ltd) • Penguin Books India Pvt Ltd, 11 Community
Centre, Panchsheel Park, New Delhi - 110 017, India • Penguin Group (NZ), 67 Apollo Drive, Rosedale, North Shore 0632, New Zealand
(a division of Pearson New Zealand Ltd) • Penguin Books (South Africa) (Pty) Ltd, • 24 Sturdee Avenue, Rosebank, Johannesburg 2196,
South Africa • Penguin Books Ltd, Registered Offices: 80 Strand, London WC2R ORL, England

Text copyright © 2010 by Sean Taylor • Illustrations copyright © 2010 by Jill Barton

Designed by Jennifer Kelly • Text set in Gothic Blond

Manufactured in China on acid-free paper

1 3 5 7 9 10 8 6 4 2

Library of Congress Cataloging-in-Publication Data
Taylor, Sean, date.
The ring went zing! : a story that ends with a kiss / by Sean Taylor ; illustrated by Jill Barton.
p. cm.
Summary: A frog, in love with a chicken, buys her a golden
ring, but when the ring falls and skips away, they begin to
chase after it, joined along the way by a jogging swan, a
motorcycling sausage dog, and other helpful creatures.

ISBN 978-0-8037-3311-4
[1. Frogs—Fiction. 2. Chickens—Fiction.
3. Animals—Fiction. 4. Love—Fiction.
5. Rings—Fiction. 6. Humorous stories.]
I. Barton, Jill, ill. II. Title.
PZ7.T21783 Rin 2009
[E]—dc22
2008001718

The art was done in pencil and watercolor.

the Ring Went Zing!

a story that ends with a kiss

By
Sean Taylor

Illustrated by
Jill Barton

DIAL BOOKS FOR YOUNG READERS
an imprint of Penguin Group (USA) Inc.

Once upon a time . . .

once and never again . . .

just once . . .

a frog and a chicken fell in love.

The frog wasn't rich. But he'd been saving up.

And now he hopped to the jeweler's shop to buy
the chicken the loveliest thing he could find.

When she saw him, the chicken sighed, "You're so handsome, it makes my heart go *BEEP BAP BOP!*"

And the frog replied, "I love you from your blinking eyes to the tips of your double-quick toes. And this, my dearest darling pie, is for you."

It was a golden ring.

But the frog was so jumpy with excitement,
and the chicken was so
woozled with love . . .

that they dropped the ring.

The frog went hopping after.

The chicken followed on the tips

of her double-quick toes.

And the ring skipped away.

(But don't worry—the story will still end with a kiss.)

Along the way, a swan was jogging.
So they hollered out,

"Please! STOP THAT RING!"

The swan looked around and gave it a stab.

She zigzagged with a backward grab.

But the ring went *ZING* and bounced away.

"Hop on!" called the swan. "We'll STOP THAT RING!"

So the frog and the chicken hopped on.

Along the way, a rabbit
was trying tricks.

So they hollered out,

"Please! STOP THAT RING!"

Diving catches were the rabbit's style.

But his diving catch missed by a mile.

The ring went *PING* and flipped away.

"Leap on!" called the rabbit. "We'll STOP THAT RING!"

So the frog, the chicken, and the swan leaped on.

Along the way, a goat was pedaling.
So they hollered out,

"Please! STOP THAT RING!"

The goat saw something whirr with a whizz.

But it came so fast, she got in a tizz.

The ring went *DING* and spun away.

"Climb on!" called the goat. "We'll STOP THAT RING!"

So the frog, the chicken, the swan, and the rabbit climbed on.

Along the way, a sausage dog was singing.
So they hollered out,

"Please, please, please!

STOP THAT RING!"

The sausage dog looked like he knew what to do.

In actual fact, he hadn't a clue.

The ring went *TING* and sprang away.

"Jump on!" called the sausage dog. "We'll STOP THAT RING!"

So the frog, the chicken, the swan, the rabbit,
and the goat jumped on.

They raced.

They chased.

They stretched.

They perched.

They hurried.

They scurried.

They swerved.

They lurched.

But the ring just kept rolling away.

On it bounced to the town square.

Then up it twisted . . . down it dropped . . . up it flicked . . . and down it plopped —

into a spouting fountain.

"It stopped!" puffed the frog.
"Up on top," huffed the dog.
"Now this story will never end
with a kiss," sighed the swan.

"Unless we try our best to do *this* . . ." chimed the chicken.

So the goat climbed the dog,
the swan climbed the goat,
the rabbit climbed the swan,
the chicken climbed the rabbit,

the frog climbed the chicken,

and he . . .

frog-hopped into the fountain.

The frog flopped this way,

rolled by the rush.

The frog spun that way,

sucked by the gush.

His friends went up on tippy-toes to see. But they
quivered . . . they teetered . . . they toppled
in a tumbledown heap.

It could have been the worst disaster the town
square had ever seen.

Instead it was the biggest burst of *laughter* the town square had ever heard. Because there, on top, was the frog . . . with the gleaming, golden ring.

(It's amazing what a frog in love will do!)

"My lovely little coochie-coo," said the frog.
"What I did, I did for you."

He gave the chicken her golden ring.

And everyone started to dance and sing.

The frog and the chicken danced cheek to cheek.

They danced toe-to-toe.

They danced mouth to beak!

And you probably think that's the kiss to end the story. **But it's not.**

Because look!